This fable is for any age...since transgender individuals come in all different ways. It will be a comfort to anyone with a transgender heart...trying to keep it together and not fall apart.

There's A Caterpillar Inside Me!

Marilyn Braude

Pictures by the author

Published by Warm Pages, Los Angeles

There's A Caterpillar Inside Me!
Marilyn Braude

This story contains the opinions and outlook of the author. The author's only purpose is to gently comfort and support those individuals already experiencing the anguish that often accompanies gender identity issues. This story is not intended to encourage anyone to change their sexual identity or to render any type of medical or professional advice.

Editor Dan D'Allaird, PsyD, LP.
Art Director Jerry Braude
Production Rebecca Mainey

Printed in the United States of America
ISBN 978-0-692-05289-1
Library of Congress Control Number 2018901511

Warm Pages Publishing · Los Angeles, California
WarmPagesPublishing@gmail.com

Table of Nonsense

Dedication

For those brave individuals who found the strength to create loving non-traditional families. I hope Butterfly's journey can help you explain, simply, why you created this special home…this special setting… this loving stage upon which your children have entered as the stars. Treasured stars.

Snow White and Cinderella legends speak only half the story. Butterfly's journey tells of those whose inner complexity has led them toward a different ending…down a difficult path only the most daring and confident can travel.

Butterfly's Prologue

I look in the mirror and what do I see?

I see someone who is not really me.

What to do? What to do?

I can either lie to myself or lie to you.

What to do? What to do?

How hard it is to live each day through

When you find your gender is not really true.

What to do? What to do?

Keep reading this book and you will see

How I solved the riddle of who I should be.

"I'm a common ordinary Mosquito.
My occupation is biting humans.
Feasting on them. I've no spare time
to be a Soothsayer. A Predictor. Still,
I predict you're not gonna believe this
tale that's about to unfold. I wouldn't
either...if I hadn't lived through it. The
thing is, our Butterfly has 'issues'...
then again, who doesn't? So don't stop
reading until you come to the very
end...but trust me, once you come to
the end, it's a waste of time to read
any farther. Actually, it's impossible."

Chapter 1

In The Far Off Distance...

lived a Tree whose top was so tall it had never been seen, except, of course, by the clever creatures who shared its many branches and bright green leaves. But this didn't mean they always agreed. They argued and bickered and hassled over both big and little things.

On one particular Leaf, a skinny Mosquito with torn ratty wings stood squabbling with a gorgeous orange Butterfly.

"Butterfly, all you do is complain. Which is crazy. You lead an easy cushy life. Those fragile fragrant flowers you sip never lean back and take fast whacks at you. But for me to eat, I'm forced to land on disgusting human feet and hands, forever dodging hits and swats that sting and smart. Look at these poor tattered Wings. Every meal I eat might be the end of me."

"So who's complaining now? Nobody told you to eat humans... to sip their yucky blood. Blood's disgusting.

"But me? You think I've had an easy life? I wasn't always as you see me now. A glorious orange Butterfly. I was, for the longest time wedged in, squeezed tight inside a gloomy damp cocoon."

"That cocoon, Butterfly, was your own silly fault. Nobody made you spin it."

"Are you kidding? One sunny day I was a happy little Caterpillar, with my pick of leaves to chew. Then wham! A voice popped on inside my head. 'Caterpillar! It's time to spin your Cocoon! Make haste!' That's all it said. Over and over and over again.

"Mosquito, trust me. I knew nothing about cocoons. Nothing. I still don't know how I finally got it spun. And now, I wish I had never got it done."

"Butterfly, you can't be telling me you want to be a little green Caterpillar again?"

"Yes, my ratty friend. I do. But once I figured how to weave myself into that cramped and dismal space, I was exhausted. A nap just happened. Looking back, I have no idea how long I slept, no way of telling time, but when I finally came awake, all my precious little feet were missing. Every single one."

"Butterfly, you're spooking me out. Feet don't just disappear. I've had these same six scrawny legs since the day I came to be."

"Mosquito, just listen to me! Worse was yet to come. Locked in that miserable cocoon, I could feel something heavy on my back. A heaviness I couldn't see or touch. I could barely breathe."

"Butterfly, you're nuts. Maybe crazy too."

"I'm not nuts, Mosquito. Just listen! My tale gets stranger still.

Somehow I made a hole in that stifling hot cocoon and wiggled free. Sitting in the sun to catch my breath and mourn my missing feet, this weight on my back gradually unfurled and became these two fantastic orange wings. They gently lifted me, and somehow, I knew how to fly. And I must confess, it was amazing to be twirling and whirling about in the sky.

"I should have been so happy. Wings can be such fun. But I missed my little legs. Every single one. For reasons I can't explain, I need to be that other me, the Caterpillar 'me' nobody else can see. Mosquito, I'm not happy being a Butterfly."

"Don't listen to that ratty Mosquito. He thinks I'm a nutcase. He can't understand how awful it is not to like the way you are made. Not to be what others see. But what can you expect from a ratty tatty Mosquito?"

Chapter 2

A Horrid Monster

As Mosquito sat pondering Butterfly's baffling tale, their glossy Leaf began to twist. Then shake.

"Mu..Muv…Move! Move back! You tu…tuu…two imbeciles. Make room for me!"

A grotesque beast, made of one big head surrounded by too many horrid legs, heaved itself up and over the edge. "One! Two! Three! Four! Five! Six! Seven! Eight! Yes Sireee. Every leg accounted for." The grotesque Beast seemed absurdly pleased.

"Who are you? What are you? Why are you counting?" Hurling these questions into the air, Mosquito and Butterfly raced to safety at the far edge of their Leaf.

"Lu…luu…look, you two jerks. I'm not in a talking mood. I'm tired. I'm starving. But this I'll explain. I've discovered it's w…wise to count my legs several times each day. Why do you think these legs do exactly as I say? I have an extra brain hidden away in every single leg. Spiders are brilliant you know."

Mosquito found his voice. "If you're so smart, why stop counting at eight?"

"Because that's all the legs I have, you idiot. Just eight. Actually,

I can count all the way to twenty-eight. If I wanted to. But if I counted past ei...eii...eight, I'd be counting nothing at all. And you can't count what isn't there. It's a waste of time. Besides, there would be no way to check if my answer is wrong or correct."

"You're lying," Mosquito snapped. "I bet you stopped at eight because eight's the highest you can count."

"You two jerks better stop talking rude to me. I'm on my way to weave a w...we...Web, the biggest Web you've ever seen. By tomorrow you'll each be nothing but a tasty meal for me."

"Spider, we're both too smart to get caught in any Web you weave," Butterfly bravely said.

"You think? Then you two numbskulls have never seen a Web like mine. I'm gonna weave it all over this Tree....from the bottom to the top. And I swear there's not a beast that flies that can unstick itself or untwist itself from a w..we..Web as strong as mine. No creature that touches it can ever come unstuck...and that's the bloody truth. Be warned. You two are doomed to die this night!"

Mosquito shivered. Butterfly stayed calm. "If you're so brilliant, why do you stutter?"

"Why do I stutter? All Spiders stutter. It's a gift. The world talks too fast...so even the biggest, best thoughts get lost. But

"Yikes! I'm stuck in this Tree. I'm stuck in this book! Maybe out in the big world, which isn't flat, everybody wouldn't hate me. I would make a wonderful friend, I think. As long as it was the kind of friend I didn't want to eat."

stuttering slows our speech and gives us time to properly think! That's why when I speak, S is never a single S to me. And T is never just one T. It takes me time to spit out my M's…but in the end, my friends, it's not my words…it's not what I say. It's the cleverness of my Webs that count in a very big way. So you two rascals had better behave."

"You're just bragging, that's all. Trying to scare us," Mosquito bravely shouted out.

"Bragging? I'm telling you two that stuttering does more to calm me down as I weave my Webs that any kind of glue. It's impossible to spin a complicated w…we..Web and not mix up so many strings without a frustrated stutter or two."

"If I were ever to spin a Web," Butterfly said, "I'd make it bright. A brilliant yellow or splendid red."

Spider smirked. "How stupid can you get. A Web that's yellow? Or even red? It can't be done."

"Who says?"

"I says. It can't be done because it's never been done. If it could've been done, it would've been done. Webs can only be sp…spun in grey. There is no other way."

"Something tells me," Butterfly replied, "you have eight legs but zero brains."

Spider roared. His belly shook. His eight legs jerked up straight. Their Leaf begin to dip, to tip, then shake, hurling the astonished Spider down into empty space.

"Good riddance," Butterfly gushed. "But still, Mosquito, we had better be careful. Even small Webs are nasty things. That horrid Spider gives me a bad feeling in my Wings."

"Don't use your wings to worry, you silly Butterfly. Just use your Wings to fly. Our fate is not something we can foresee. Both good and bad and everything in between, either comes or doesn't come to be. It's hard enough to jiggle and juggle the present. So let the future be."

Chapter **3**

Toes: A Private Conversation

Watching Spider's dangerous unexpected exit, Mosquito's head began to tilt. Right to left. Left to right.

"I'm dizzy…real dizzy. Butterfly, come help. That creepy Spider has given me the Tilts.

"I'm dizzy too. I must have caught the Tilting sickness from that ghastly Spider too."

"Butterfly," Mosquito said as he tried to steady his tilting head, "you don't have the Tilts. It's a known fact Butterflies don't get dizzy."

"We do too. I'm even too dizzy to fly. I may be terribly ill. And a lot you care. Worse, suppose that dastardly Spider meant what he said? With our tilting heads, and without any toes to save us, we may both wind up in his horrid Web…watching, helpless while that ghastly Spider slowly sucks out all our blood."

"Butterfly, what are you talking about? What have toes to do with anything? Toes are only half made fingers sticking out of human feet."

"Trust me, Mosquito, I know what I know. Humans have knees. We have knees. They have hips and so do we. But toes? Neither you nor me have any toes. Not a single one. And since

I've never seen a human get trapped in any Web, the answer is obvious. They have toes!"

Mosquito glanced down at his own spindly legs. "Ye Gads! You're right! I don't have any toes. My legs just end."

"Isn't that what I just said? This is why we can get so easily trapped in even the smallest harmless Web."

"What a horrible evil way for my tiny life to end! But you must be right. Without toes, we are doomed!"

"Mosquito, that's what I've been saying. You need to focus more."

Staring at his toeless legs again, Mosquito began adding up everything Butterfly said.

"Butterfly, I've bitten hundreds of human feet. In fact, toes are one of the tastiest meals I eat. But even the biggest feet I've landed on and dined upon, only have five toes each."

"That's because humans only need to grow a total of ten toes, to gain enough speed to escape those horrid Webs that so easily capture you and me. Remember, I was once a Caterpillar with many fancy feet. But as fast as Caterpillars sometimes go, I was still always somewhat slow. I finally discovered my tardiness was because I didn't own a single toe.

"And since you and me are missing toes, for reasons nobody

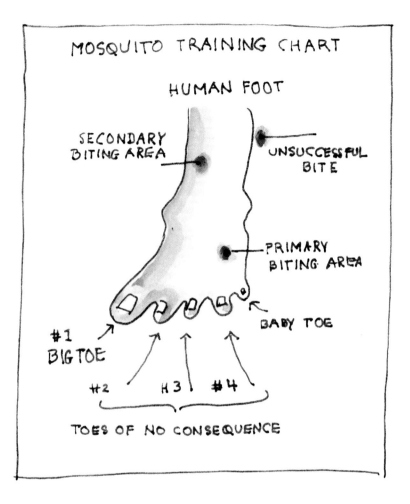

MOSQUITO TRAINING CHART

HUMAN FOOT

SECONDARY BITING AREA

UNSUCCESSFUL BITE

PRIMARY BITING AREA

BABY TOE

#1 BIG TOE

#2　#3　#4

TOES OF NO CONSEQUENCE

even knows, we must both watch carefully for that horrid Spider's very next Web. He is a most dangerous enemy. Mosquito, are you listening? Are you hearing me? I'm telling you all this because I'm getting another bad feeling in my Wings."

"Butterfly, your Wings look fine to me. It's a waste of time to fret about what hasn't happened yet and may never come to be. Remember, the future always follows both the Present and the Past. The Future always happens last."

Chapter 4

Names

"Butterfly, since we both like living on this Leaf, I guess introductions are in order. I have to call you something. So I had better learn your name."

"Names, Mosquito? I can't think about introductions now! What if that horrid Spider comes back!"

"Butterfly, this Tree has a million leaves. Even if he really has a brain hidden away in every leg, he's still not smart enough to once again climb up and find our special Leaf."

"Even so, Mosquito, we still have a problem. A big one."

"We do? How can we have a problem now that ghastly Spider is gone?"

"We have a problem, Mosquito, because I don't have a name. We can't be introduced. You'll never be able to call me anything at all."

"No name? That's impossible, Butterfly. Are you trying to be rude?"

"Rude? No way. But listen closely, Mosquito, while I explain. I can't give myself a name because I'm all confused. I don't know yet just who I am...a Caterpillar or a Butterfly. And it's obvious Caterpillars and Butterflies need very different kinds of names."

"You're a Butterfly," Mosquito remarked, studying his new companion closely. "No doubt about it."

"I know, Mosquito, I'm a Butterfly on the outside. But there is lots of a shy green Caterpillar still inside of me…which is why I am constantly missing all my little feet….and all the delicious leaves I use to eat. So first I must figure out who I was meant to be. What I really am. My graceful shape and lovely Wings fool not only strangers, but sometimes they fool me. But enough of my worries, Mosquito. What name do you go by?"

Mosquito paused. "You may not believe me, Butterfly, but Mosquitoes don't have names. There are far too many of us. When summer comes and the Sun shines hot, millions of my companions come to be each day. And it's quite obvious there are not a million names.

"If we wanted names, thousands of us would have to agree to share a name that is the same. Which would put us all in a pickle."

"So why not numbers? You can never run out of numbers. Numbers go on forever. Even I, a simple Butterfly on the outside, know this to be a fact."

"Yes, Butterfly…but numbers are so impersonal. So cold.

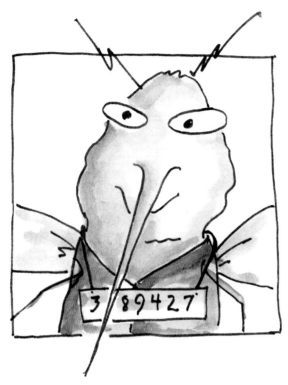

"I know what I know. It doesn't matter what anyone calls me. A name can't change me. A name can't make me any better or any worse. I am what I am. But don't try telling this to our Butterfly. She thinks she is what she isn't... or isn't what she is. Now she's got me all mixed up!"

Whether you decide you are a Caterpillar or a Butterfly, would you want to be called a number? Numbers are humbling. Worse yet, some bully Mosquito with a big number might get the idea he is more important than some poor Mosquito whose name is only 'One' or 'Two'. So you see, Butterfly, with so many of us, we're pretty much stuck."

Butterfly closed her eyes. "We're stuck is right. Stuck together on this wondrous Leaf. So if it's OK with you Mosquito...I guess we skip the names?"

"Butterfly," Mosquito replied, flapping his shabby wings, "how very clever you are...whatever it is...that is...you are."

Chapter **5**

The Snail

Meanwhile Spider was falling fast. Gaining speed. "Curses on that Mosquito and Butterfly! I'm doomed. I'm about to c...cr...crack my head! I might even break a leg or two... maybe all eight if I can't land perfectly straight."

Still spitting out these frantic shouts, Spider crashed... belly first...legs sprawled out...upon a startled creature made of just two parts.

The creature's bottom half had two sticks that protruded out on different sides and held its tiny eyes, but there were no legs or ears or hands anywhere about. It was just an unfinished blob that somehow slid along. The small brown shell that sat atop its back, faithfully followed this bottom half.

"Dang it! Dang it all! What just landed on my back?" Twisting the sticks that held its eyes, the simple creature beheld a horrid guest, a ghastly beast with too many feet. "Introduce yourself! Who are you? What are you? And get off my back! It's a miracle you didn't break me smack in half!!"

"What am I? A stupid question only a two-part creature would ask. I know precisely what I am. The big question is... what are you? And where did you leave your feet?"

"Feet? What would I do with feet? I'm a Snail. So most of me is a single foot. A walking tool. I can get anywhere I want just the way I'm made. Which is why I can't figure why you have so many legs. Don't they tangle and get in each other's way?"

"Nope. Never. I have a hidden brain in every leg. So each of my legs knows how to behave. Both the four on my left and the four on my right know precisely when to stop and when to start."

"Four and four is eight! You have eight legs? Not nine or seven? Ye gads! This means you are a Spider! One of those horrid creatures that spin ghastly Webs of grey…Webs that do your dirty work…that trap and capture all your prey. While poor Snails like me, tired as we might be, must always keep sliding and slipping along to slowly reach even a skimpy meal of soggy leaves."

"Facts are facts, Snail. It's obvious, by the time you get anywhere, the food is no longer there. As the ancient saying goes, 'The last to arrive doesn't dine.' Now let me to show you how fast well-trained legs should go."

"Don't bother. I am quite happy the way I am made. My single foot goes very slow, I know, because it has to pull the heavy load of slime I carry deep inside me, everywhere I go. You

"Yuk! I can't stand Spiders! And one just landed on my back! And a rude one at that! Gads! I need a bath. But I can't. If any water gets inside my shiny shell, it might rinse away my entire supply of silver slime. I couldn't stand that."

have no idea how very hard it is to slip and slide ahead and still leave behind a beautiful trail of silver slime."

"If it's such a burden, why bother?"

"Why bother? Are you crazy? When I want to go back the way I came, I just slide along my very own trail of slippery slime. See how clever Snails can be? How brilliantly we think?"

"Slime trails are disgusting"

"So are Spiders. Now get off my back! Take your eight ugly legs and go away. Go far away."

"Go away? Go far away? I'm already gone you conceited creep. I've better things to do than sit up here on top of you. I'm off to spin a giant Web all over this lofty Tree that towers high above both you and me. While toppling from one of its highest leaves, my fall took so long, I had time to devise a brilliant new Web design. I shall be the first Spider to ever catch me a human."

"Spider, your fancy Web won't work. When humans aren't being stupid, they can be pretty smart."

"If my Web doesn't work, and my human escapes, then I'll dine on a ratty Mosquito and Orange Butterfly tonight."

"Which will you eat first?"

"What a question! Snail, I have no idea. That tattered Mosquito I have in mind is half starved…not much meat on him anywhere. Then again, I've never tasted a Butterfly. Her orange Wings might be too brittle and too dry. But not to worry. With any l…lu…luck and my fabulous new Web design, I shall be dining on a succulent human tonight."

"Good luck to you, Spider. Just don't erase any of my lovely trails of silver slime."

"Not to worry. Now I'm off!" Jumping down from the Snail's lopsided shell, the Spider waved his two favorite legs. "Be grateful Snail, you aren't the kind of tasty morsel Spiders like to eat, or I might be dining on you tonight."

The Snail stared hard at Spider's departing shape. "I wonder how that Spider taught his two front legs to wave. They are exceptionally well trained."

Chapter **6**

The Grey Worm Arrives

"Hey, Butterfly! Come quick. A wiggly Grey Worm has somehow climbed our Tree and is attempting to get on our Leaf! Should I push him off?"

"Mosquito, are you nuts? Worms bring good luck."

"Who told you that?"

"Nobody told me. It's just something all Butterflies know. Now help me pull him up onto our Leaf."

"And exactly how? Look for yourself. This simple creature has no hands. No feet. How in the heck do you suppose he grabs his food to eat?"

"Mosquito, that's his problem. Not ours. Now stand back while he wiggles up over the edge."

The Grey Worm heaved himself onto their Leaf. He was a dirty shade of somber grey. Not too thin and not too long. An opening for a mouth. But nothing more. Mosquito was right. No hands. No feet. Not even a single row of teeth.

Mosquito was stumped. "How can you eat without any teeth?"

"How can I eat? How do you eat? Have you looked properly at yourself? You don't have any teeth either."

"But I have this clever built-in straw to sip my meals," Mosquito explained, showing the Worm how his proboscis looked both from the front and from the side. "And my pal here with the big orange Wings has one of these clever sipping straws too. But you, poor Worm, have nothing. What do you do? How do you chew?"

The Worm did not answer immediately. He pondered. Then slowly he opened his mouth very wide so both the Mosquito and Butterfly could peer inside. They couldn't see anything but a deep tunnel that led far down into the darkest dark.

The Grey Worm closed its mouth. Then opened it, but not quite so wide this time. "I don't fool around. I never dawdle. I am a genius at swallowing. There is very little dirt I don't know how to swallow. But I admit, if I had teeth, I could allow myself a few extra treats. Dirt, you know is a most boring monotonous diet."

"It's a shame you can't sip a bit of blood. Blood is so delicious. So refreshing. So sustaining."

"If he sips anything," Butterfly countered, "it should be the sweet nectar all the flowers save for me. Nothing can surpass its mellow richness. By the way, Worm, just what are you doing in our Tree, and on our Leaf? You should be buried in the ground."

"I know. I know. But it is so boring day after day in the ground. Nothing to do but wiggle and squiggle and eat the same old dirt. I know I am just a lowly worm. But even Worms can dream. I'm tired of nothing but dirt. I want to breathe fresh air. I want to see the sky. As a matter of fact, I'm on my way up to touch it."

Butterfly stretched her Wings. They were quite dazzling. "You would have to climb to the very tippy top of our Tree to touch the sky. It is a vast undertaking for a lowly Worm. And a dangerous one. I myself would never attempt it. Even with these wondrous Wings."

"Me, neither," Mosquito added in. They all looked up. It was indeed a very tall Tree. They could barely see its tip that was far above and very high. "Worm, think twice. You are attempting a terribly steep and dangerous climb."

"A very scary climb." Butterfly was concerned. "Worm, look at yourself. You have no hands or feet. Your skin will get covered with sickly sores and dreadful cuts. Are you sure it's worth it? Can't you be happy just watching the sky from here on our Leaf which isn't too low and isn't too high?"

The Grey Worm grew still. And quiet. He stared up at the sky. He looked down at the ground. His companions waited.

"I know you think I'm just a lowly Worm. But I am a genius at swallowing. I can swallow any kind of dirt I see. But of course, I would enjoy my meals far more if I had a row of pretty teeth. I could chop my food..and grind my food...and really have a feast. But maybe then...I wouldn't be a Worm? Now I'm all confused."

"I know if I climb to the top of this Tree, it will probably be the end of me. But I am so tired of living in the dirt...I'm determined to reach the top of this Tree. Nothing can stop me now. Farewell my friends."

Slowly, quietly, the Grey Worm once again began his climb. Both Mosquito and Butterfly watched as he grew small, then smaller, than smallest. Then disappeared.

"Do you think he'll make it?"

Butterfly closed her lovely eyes. "We may never know. But wow! That Worm has nerve. Me thinks it's not the top of the Tree that matters to that lowly Worm anyhow. Not at all. It's the excitement of the climb. Long live our Worm!

"But drat! Oh drat! Mosquito, I forgot to tell him about that horrid Spider's cunning plan. I should have warned him. What do lowly Worms know of Webs? Now I'm getting another bad feeling in my Wings."

"Butterfly, stop imagining terrible things. What is meant to be, will be. What isn't meant to be, can't ever come to be. It's foolish to worry about what isn't here and may never appear. Trust me. Ignore your foolish Wings."

Chapter 7

The Poet

"Stop! Stop! You're going to tip us both off!" Butterfly was hanging on as Mosquito leaned dangerously out over the edge of their Leaf, bending as far as he could go.

"Butterfly! Come quick! You gotta see this. You gotta see this crazy Snake. He's reciting poetry. From memory. Must be off his rocker. No…off his rattles. Ha Ha! Too much sitting in the hot Sun, I think."

"My brilliant method of locomotion, called slithering, was invented the same day Snakes were invented. Slithering is a highly advanced form of locomotion, excusing all Snakes from the necessity of needing those clumsy appendages called legs. But are we admired? Respected? Valued? Esteemed? Nope. None of the above. Nobody appreciates the art of slithering. Nobody. That's why I want some feet. And fast."

"I'm not leaning out over any edge, just to listen to some Snake blabbering poems. What's he reciting anyway?"

"Far-out stuff. His words are crystal clear. All the way up here. It's his thoughts that are all garbled."

"I want two hands and I want two feet. I want to hold the creatures I eat."

The Snake continued his recital.

"I want to stand. I don't want to crawl. Nobody can see I'm the best creature of all."

The Snake took a quick break to rattle his rattles, then proudly continued on.

"I'm tired of slithering without any feet. I'm tired of the crummy creatures I have to eat."

This flow of poetry stopped suddenly. Butterfly was perplexed, but still refused to look down. "So why all the quiet? What's happening now?"

"Not sure," Mosquito replied, leaning still farther over the Leaf. "The Snake's gone…spotted a tired mouse far off in the distance. Took off after it…that's my best guess. Even great poets have to eat."

Chapter 8

Spider Returns

Mosquito and Butterfly had somehow now become the best of friends. In the midst of this quiet and calm, their glossy green Leaf, once more, began to wobble and shake as that dreaded Spider, leg by ugly leg, yet again took over their peaceful space.

"Good grief! How did you find your way back?" Mosquito was aghast.

"I told you, I've got a brain in every leg. Now I'm back to catch me a roly-poly human, plump and wide…one meal to last me my entire lifetime. That's it. In a nutshell."

"Catch a human? In a Web? Impossible. It can't be done."

"And just why not?" Spider's temper began to ignite. "You think those humans are too s…sm…smart for me? Me with an extra brain in every leg?"

"It's not their smartness," Butterfly explained. "Everyone knows their smartness comes and goes. But have you even studied one up close? Humans are not only huge walking beasts. And as I've explained, they all have ten toes each. They can escape any Web you weave. At least all the humans I've ever seen."

"I've been told the Octopus has ei..eight legs just like me. I've never met an Octopus. But they are supposed to be very smart too. But I can't be sure if they have an extra b...br...brain in every leg, like I'm positive I do. Even if nobody believes me, I know it's true."

"Toes. Schmoes. You both just watch m..me...me and see."

Tipping one of his long ugly legs to his horrendously big head, the frenzied Spider jumped off their Leaf to a leaf far beyond, and deftly began his plan. He worked with amazing speed. Quietly and quickly an enormous Web began to take shape. It was everywhere. From the ground to the top of their Tree. But you had to look closely or it couldn't be seen.

As Spider stood back to admire his dazzling skill and speed, Mosquito asked, "Tell me again how this ghastly Web is suppose to work?"

"Easy as pie. I just sit back now and wait for some human, hopefully a roly-poly human, to wander by. I know for sure there isn't a person alive that can escape this wondrous w…we.. Web I have cleverly woven and brilliantly designed."

Differences forgotten, Spider, Butterfly, and Mosquito sat back to wait, but each at a different edge of their Leaf. Just as their patience grew thin, a ten-toed human, fat not trim, could be vaguely seen in the dim far distance. He started off small but grew bigger and bigger and rounder and rounder as he came closer and closer to his dreadful fate.

Finally, finally, at last, right in front of Mosquito and Butterfly and Spider's goggling eyes, this roly-poly ten-toed human walked smack into Spider's giant sprawling gossamer Web. But rather than being trapped, imprisoned, immobilized, this roly-poly human just kept on walking…casually tossing the world's largest, most dangerous Web aside.

"D…d…Drat! And double drat! And more than that!" Spider studied his broken brilliant Web. "All my work for nothing. I'm exhausted. I'm hungry. But I'm still a genius. I'm going to bed."

"Spider! Wait! You can't sleep here!" Mosquito too was now in a most foul mood. "There isn't room. So scram. Skedaddle. Skadoooo."

"Butterfly, I'm too tired to move. But not to worry. I only have time for a quick short snooze. Then I'm off! And if either of you rascals wake me up, I'll spin a circular Web around this Leaf and eat the two of you all up tonight! And that's a p..pr...promise!"

Mosquito somberly watched their snoring guest. "I've a great idea. Butterfly, you grab four legs and I'll grab four...and if we lift together we can toss him over the edge."

"Never! Never! Ever! I've never touched a Spider before. And I'm not about to begin. So I guess we must let him stay. While he's ugly as sin, he's not really all that big. But we must watch out for that next Web he's threatened to spin. I have a bad feeling in my Wings."

"Butterfly, ignore your Wings. I've told you this before. And I'll say it again. 'We can't see the Future until it becomes the Present then the Past. We always see the Future last.'"

"I know. I know. But it's all so unfair."

"Butterfly, if we could see the Future first, we'd have no way of knowing when we go someplace, if we are getting there early or way too late."

"Mosquito, you are either far smarter or a lot dumber than you appear...or act...or think. But I guess I'm kinda glad you're with me on this Leaf. I think..."

Chapter **9**

The Ant Visits

Busy watching the unwanted Spider snore and sleep, legs all askew, Butterfly almost stepped on a most unusual creature sprawled flat out upon their Leaf.

"Mosquito. Come quick! Tell me what this odd poorly proportioned creature can be? And just how many uninvited guests do you think we can we squeeze on our Leaf?"

This newest arrival opened its eyes. Twisted its too big head from left to right. "There is plenty of room on this Leaf for me. I'm long but very thin." Spitting this sentence out, their narrow visitor now began to tremble, then sob. Big wide sobs. Not the long thin sobs that should have spilled out.

Butterfly leaned down. "What's wrong? Mop up your tears and tell me who you are. And what you are. You have a most odd shape. You dip in way too far at the waist. You aren't by any chance a Wasp?"

"You've just insulted me. Wasps are mean and frightful things. I am a peaceful Ant. That's what I am. I was born an Ant. So an Ant I shall always be. Everyone knows you can never change what you are, not once you have been fully made."

"You are all the way wrong. Dead wrong. Just look at me. A Butterfly is what you see. But Butterflies are never born. We simply 'come to be'. I was born a Caterpillar…a most beautiful shade of green. Then one day, I was forced to spin a small cocoon, and I must tell you, cocoons are very hard to do. So I promptly fell into a deep and somber sleep. When I finally came awake, I discovered Somebody, somehow, had stolen all my legs…and made me into this Butterfly you see, complete with these enormous Wings. But I'd change these Wings in a minute to get back all my little feet."

"Are you nuts, Butterfly? Wanting crummy feet instead of gorgeous Wings? Nobody sane would want to be a homely Caterpillar when they could be a pretty Butterfly."

"Ant, you just don't understand. The inside 'me' is very different from the outside 'me' you see. I'm desperate to figure out which is the real true me."

"Butterfly, you're crazy. Or seriously sick. Or hallucinating. Or maybe a touch of all three."

"Ant! You're mind is stuck shut. And your ears too. You're not listening to me, hearing me, when I try to explain to you how I feel more like a Caterpillar than a Butterfly. So scram! Skedaddle! Your head is too big and your mind is too thin. So go. Get off my nice clean Leaf!"

"Don't send me away. I've no place to go. I have no home. You

see, I stopped for a second to look up at the Sky, and the long
Ant line I was marching in, kept right on marching and passed
me by. Not a single Ant would let me back in line. Trust me
friend. I asked. I tried."

"Well that was a stupid thing to do," mumbled Mosquito
from his side of the Leaf. "Why would anyone want to look
up at the Sky?"

"Drat! I finally get up
the courage to step
out of my endless
Ant line...and who do
I meet? A Butterfly
who isn't even sure
if she's a Butterfly.
I thought everybody
knew what they were.
I know I'm an Ant.
And that's that."

"Because it never ends. The Sky is vast. The Sky is wide. And while I'm marching in line I like to gaze up and try to understand how me, a tiny Ant, ever came to be…and if there is some big Grand Plan. I know I can puzzle this all out. While my waist is tiny, my head is huge. And my mind is huge too. But thinking vast thoughts takes time, and I'm always marching, marching, marching in long straight lines…marching marching all the time."

A fast answer flew from Mosquito's lips. "You're talking nonsense. And thinking nonsense too. We're just here. That's it. There is no marvelous Scheme or Plan. Life is work. It's hunger and it's thirst. I'm not surprised the other Ants wouldn't let you back in their perfect line."

The Ant shot back. "You could be right. You could be wrong. But in my humble Ant opinion, Mosquitoes eat, but do not think. Apparently, proper thinking can only be properly done by a brilliant Ant, like me."

"Little Ant," Mosquito advised, "don't waste your time staring up at the endless Sky for answers that are too hard for a narrow Ant to find. You are better off doing what Ants do best. Marching in long straight lines looking for fallen creatures and crumbs upon which to dine."

Instead of refuting this dreadful fact, the Ant tipped over and fell flat on its back…motionless. Silent. Still. As Mosquito and Butterfly leaned over to see if their guest was alive, the Ant jumped up. "Stand back! Stand back, I say."

"Are you alright?"

"Am I alright? No I'm not alright. I have amnesia and can't remember a single word I said. I must have fallen and bumped my head. I'm not even sure how I got on this Leaf."

Just then, they heard yelling from down below…from a voice the thin brilliant Ant seemed to know. "That's my best friend. He's in line behind me everyday. 'Hey Sheldon! I'm way up here. Look up! It's me. Is that you down there?' "

"Of course it's me. Who else would it be? I finally got them to hold up the line. But they won't wait forever. You better come quick."

"I'm coming. I'm coming." And bending from it's tiny waist, the narrow Ant made a courtly bow. "I've got to go. I've got to eat. Maybe someday I'll remember all that happened on this Leaf."

Chapter 10

The Climber

Hands behind her Wings. Feet forward. Back and forth. Forth and back. From one end of the Leaf to the other.

"Butterfly! Stop that dreadful pacing. You're making me crazy. Why are you pacing anyway?"

"Mosquito, it's that foolish Worm. I can't squeeze him out of my mind. Poor fellow. He can't possibly make it to the top of our Tree. I should have begged him not to go. He may easily freeze or faint from cold."

As Butterfly was spilling these dismal words, something, a shapeless something, fell from the sky landing half conscious in the center of their Leaf. Whatever it was, it didn't move. Didn't speak. Just lay dazed at Mosquito's feet.

"Butterfly! Come quick! Come look! What can this strange shape be?"

"Mosquito, it's our Worm. Frayed to smithereens. Poor thing."

As Butterfly and Mosquito bent over their fragile friend, fearing to see a tragic end, its tangled body shivered, then wiggled wide awake. The Worm gazed happily up. "My friends! If I had arms I'd hug you both…never thought I'd see you two again."

Giving their injured guest no chance to speak, both together said, "Tell us…did you get to the top?"

The Worm gave a pitiful shrug. "I had just made it past these dreadful Ants, when I heard from behind thunder and rumbling of a savage kind. As I turned back to look, I could see a brutish beast, made of just one hideous head surrounded by hundreds of gangling legs. And all these dangerous hideous legs were racing up our Tree…coming fast and straight at me.

"It was the most savage fiend I had ever seen…even though… as it came close…I could see nowhere near a hundred legs… just eight. But those eight were traveling at a frightening speed.

"This Beast was practically on top of me, when it yelled, 'M…Move! Move over! I'm on my way to the top! I've no time to stop!'"

"I tried hard to wiggle out of its way, but even a fast wiggle can take me all day. So this Monster screamed to all of its feet, 'S…st…Stop! Stop! You idiots stop! And believe it or not, all eight legs instantly obeyed. My life was saved.

"But I was still trembling and terribly afraid. I cringed as his angry eyes studied me from between all his feet. I couldn't even find the demon's mouth when it started to speak. 'Odd creature. Where are you from? It looks to me like you are only part way done. It's impossible to tell which is your Head and which is your End. Enlighten me.'"

"I'm all the way done. I'm only what you see. This is all there is of me. This is the way I'm supposed to be."

"Creature you are teasing me. Tell me again. Are you made of just one head and just one end? Or maybe two heads and not any ends? Then again, maybe you have two ends and are missing a head?"

"Spider, I have just one Head and just one End. This is the way all Worms are made. And I'm quite happy as I am."

The gross Monster used one of it's many legs to scratch its great round waist. "If you are certain you are all the way done, then let's the t..tw..two of us have some fun. Race me up to the top of this Tree!"

"What do you take me for? Do I look dumb? If you look close, you'll see I don't have any hands and I don't have any feet. There is no way I can compete. Eight legs against none? This race is fixed. It's dishonest and illegal because you've already won. And it hasn't begun.

"Sensing my wrath, the ungainly Beast changed its tune."

"No r...ra...race today? So I guess that's OK. But creature, at least tell me where you are from...where creatures are considered finished when they are only half way done."

"I'm battered. I'm beat. I'm a mess. But I did it! I touched the sky! At least I think I did. But I'd better confess...I couldn't feel it. First I touched it with the end that's my head. When nothing happened, I touched it with the end that's my end. I really tried."

"I didn't like his snotty stuttering words. But I held my temper and proudly said, 'I am an ordinary Garden Worm. I come from a wondrous land called Dirt.'"

"And where is this marvelous land called Dirt?"

"My land of Dirt is inside the Earth. This is where I'm from."

"You can't f..f...fool me. I have a brain in every leg. And nothing lives in the Dirt. It's empty. I've spent a lifetime building Webs all over it. And I know what I know. There is nothing below."

"You may know what you know. This may be so. But it's also impossible to know what you have never learned, which is, my land of Dirt is filled with worms. I'm telling you, Spider, Dirt is a busy place to be…filled with rocks and roots and a million zillion creatures just like me."

"Worm, you're making your facts all up. Hallucinating. Fantasizing. Now do you want to race to the top of our Tree? Or not? Yes or no?"

"I would have to borrow four of your legs to make our race fair."

"What a silly Worm you are. I think you have two ends and not a single head. Legs don't come off. They can't be shared. But I'll tell you what I'll do. I'll give you a big head start. Let me take my two favorite feet and push you up the hardest part."

"Don't touch me. Don't come near."

Looking up at Mosquito and Butterfly, the poor Worm wailed, "The thought of touching a Spider is one of my very worst fears. I got so afraid, I lost my grip and fell all the way back down to here. But I cannot stay.

"As I was telling that horrid Spider all the glories of the Dirt, I realized my desire to climb is through. It's gone. Now I just want to go home. At home, my friends all know which of my ends is my Head. And which of my ends is my End. I miss my home. I miss my friends."

With these fateful words, the Worm wiggled and squiggled and squirmed off their Leaf…headed in a deliberate, fantastic free fall dive back to his precious land of Dirt.

"Did you see that brazen leap, Mosquito? What a Worm! What a Worm! Me thinks…tucked in between his Head and his End… hidden somewhere in the middle, sits a very brave big heart. Which proves, once again, we are so much more than just the sum of our 'seeable' parts."

Chapter 11

A Frog Lands

"Finally, at last, I can relax," said Mosquito to nobody in particular, just as something green and damp crashed smack, dead center, into this busy Leaf.

The newcomer sat stunned. "Where am I? And what do you suppose these are?"

"You idiot! Those are your very own legs." Mosquito had never encountered such ignorance before. "What do you think? That they belong to somebody else? You must have landed on your head, or be off your rocker, not to know these legs are yours. Just what is your problem?"

"My problem? My problem? These two monstrous legs are my problem. That is, if they are actually mine, as you insist they are. Then again, if they aren't mine and belong to somebody else…then I have no problem. Somebody else has my problem."

"You are a Frog. Frogs all have ghastly big legs."

"Then I don't want to be a Frog. I want to be a tadpole again. I was such a cute little guy. Swimming about. Happy as a tadpole can get. Then slowly, quietly, my perfect tadpole body began to change on me. Look at these two ghastly legs. I would never have ordered these!

"This Tree is a crazy place for a Frog with a fear of heights to be...stuck half way up in the sky with an obnoxious Mosquito and mixed-up Butterfly. I may be stuck up here forever, because these monstrous legs never do what I tell them to. They never do what I say. I am not a happy Frog."

"And even worse, they are poorly trained. They make me jump when I want to sit. They make me hop when I want to rest. Now look where they have taken me...all the way up here...into your stupid Tree where I don't belong and don't want to be. I want to be a tadpole again. I want to be me."

"That's not about to happen Frog. I can give you one big guarantee. And anyway, you should be happy to be a Frog and have these monstrous legs." Mosquito looked down at his own skinny feet. "If I had such fabulous legs I would never ever complain."

"You can have them for all I care. But they won't come off. I've tried. They are both stuck tight. I can't see any glue to break or strings to untie, or I would leave them very far behind. Which puts me in a dreadful bind. A magnificent old Frog I bumped into, while I was busy trying to pull them off one day, took one look and told me I'd never be a tadpole again…that these horrid legs were here to stay.

"He said Nature did it, and what Nature sticks…never comes unstuck."

"And you believed him?"

"Well…Mosquito, he looked very smart."

'Frog, it's possible to look smart and be stupid…and to be stupid but look smart. It happens all the time."

"I didn't think of that."

"It seems to me, Froggie, you weren't thinking at all. But on the assumption he might be correct, and you truly own these monstrous things, then I say just enjoy them. They're really quite spectacular. With just a little patience you could train them to behave."

"But, Mosquito, I would never have chosen these legs for my own. Look how big and complicated they are. They never do what I say. They make me take great leaps…when I want a tiny jump. Watch. I'll show you how I have to fold them up every single time I want to go someplace." In the next instant, the Frog was gone. All the way gone.

Mosquito, studying his own shabby feet, couldn't believe the speed at which the Frog sailed off. "How can that Frog not love those legs? If I had legs like his I would never complain. If this Nature fellow ever lands on our Leaf, I'm going to ask how to improve my own skinny feet."

"That's fine for you, Mosquito. But I'm going to ask where in the world my own little Caterpillar feet could be. I miss every single one. Those little legs of mine faithfully carried me to dine upon all my favorite leaves and vines."

"You used to eat leaves? Gads! You would already have gobbled our Leaf all up…and then where would we both be? You'd better stick to being a Butterfly."

Butterfly studied their glossy green Leaf. "You know Mosquito, this Leaf doesn't even appeal to me. Oh, I am so mixed up. It's awful to be all confused about who you are and what you were meant to be. I'm so much more than the simple Butterfly everybody sees. There is lots of wondrous Caterpillar still inside of me. But nobody can glimpse this other me. They only see my shimmering Wings.

"I am such an unhappy Butterfly."

Chapter 12

Spider's Nap Is Over

The snoring abruptly stopped. Eight long legs flipped and flopped.

"Spider! Wake up! Get up!" Mosquito was yelling from across the Leaf, since he had no intention of getting any closer. "Get up! Be gone! Get off our Leaf!"

"I'm not leaving 'til I count my legs. I don't d..d..dare leave even one leg behind."

"Spider, are you out of your cunning mind? Nobody loses their legs when they sleep. Just the idea gives me the creeps."

"I did!" Butterfly chimed in. "They were so beautiful..those perfect little legs I had. Of course, I didn't exactly lose them. They were stolen. I was robbed! But Spider, your case is all different. Nobody in their right mind would steal long creepy Spider legs."

"You're wrong. Both of you. My legs are miraculous. In high demand. Have you ever heard of a Spider falling from his Web? Never! Not ever! So any creature who has a Web might very well try to steal a leg or two of mine."

"Well I don't have a Web. And my Mosquito friend here doesn't either. So we don't want your legs. They're disgusting. And

"Trying to explain simple math to imbeciles has tuckered me out. I need a nap. I'm going to dream I'm spinning a Web so big...it will cover the land and cover the sea...it will easily cover this big tall Tree...and trap that snotty Mosquito and Butterfly for me. I'll tie them up and gobble them up...and enjoy a feast fit for a Spider as clever as me."

anyway, we both have wings to fly, even if Mosquito's skimpy wings aren't big and beautiful like mine."

"Well, I'm not traveling anywhere 'til I count them. Nothing personal, but I don't trust anybody at all." Spider then turned back to continue his work. "Ah Ha! I still have eight. And eight, you know, is a m...ma..magical number."

"How so? Eight is only eight. One less than nine. Two less than ten."

"You are missing the significance of eight. Eight is made of two tiny zeros. One on top and one below. Two nothings. And yet, when you stack these two nothings, it is not double nothing. It is eight! Four twos. Two fours. But remember, side by side they mean nothing. Two zeros are only magical when they are properly stacked. But I forgive your stupidity. It is very difficult for a simple Mosquito and Butterfly to properly understand complicated higher math."

Both Mosquito and Butterfly studied Spider's speech. Twisted it around inside their heads. But only Mosquito spoke up. "Your reasoning is stupid. One nothing and one nothing can only ever amount to two of nothing, even stacked. And we don't need anybody on our Leaf who does such unethical flimsy math."

Not listening to Mosquito's rant, Spider twisted his big heavy head. "What's that strange rumble. It's rumbling underneath my feet and I can feel it rumbling across each and every Leaf."

"Beats me," Butterfly replied. "But somehow, strange as it may seem, I think maybe our Tree is trying to speak."

Chapter 13

The Tree Speaks

"Shut up! Shut up! You down there on my Leaf. I can't do any thinking with your nonsense and noise. If you can't be quiet, go away. Go far away. Stop messing up my busy day."

Spider looked up. "I'm not budging. Counting all my legs has e…ex…exhausted me."

"I heard what you said," the Tree shouted down.

"I don't believe this! Trees can speak?" Spider's eyes were spinning.

"Of course Trees can talk. We just can't walk. But we can think. We don't just stand around…doing nothing…even with roots that keep us stuck in the ground. Trust me. I think great thoughts…and after I think them…I whisper them into the wind, which then carries off…even my heaviest most important thoughts."

Spider's eyes kept spinning. "Tree, pardon my s…st..stupidity. But curiosity has the best of me. Since Trees can speak, I've got to ask, do you ever sleep?"

"Sleep? How can I sleep? With your noisy chattering all around and the constant worry I might get chopped down? You couldn't sleep either if you were me. If you were a Tree. With these deep roots of mine, I can't run off and cleverly hide or find some kind of brilliant disguise. Trust me. I've tried."

"Tree, stay calm. You're way too big and forbidding to get all chopped down then all chopped up."

"Spider, you don't know humans the way I do. It's hard to explain, but humans have this thing for cutting down the biggest and most beautiful trees. They may want a road. They may want our wood. Or they may not like our leaves. The human mind is not too easily understood. Humans do not always think as clearly as they should.

"But Spider, don't worry over me. I've lived long enough to know it is possible to find bits of happiness tucked here and there inside of sadness. During my sleepless nights, while wide awake and standing tall, I do my most important thinking. It's just too bad my thoughts are all invisible. Even my biggest ones. So all anybody sees when they look at me is just a tall and silent Tree."

"How much thinking can a big Tree like you really do?"

"Spider, I'll tell you exactly how much thinking a smart Tree like me can do. I am so tall, I reach so high, most of me is in the sky. This great height allows me to observe the Sun most carefully. And I've discovered each morning, precisely at dawn, our giant Sun begins its heavy climb all the way to the top of the sky.

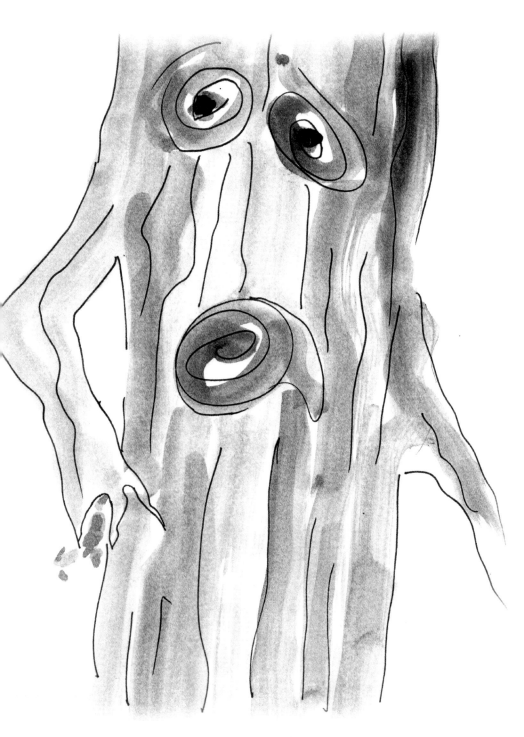

"There is very little a Tree can do except let the various creatures
crawl all over you. There have been so many creatures over
time, most have fallen from my mind. Except for one or two..."

"But it takes some kind of nudge to make anything go. I've studied enough science to know this is so. Nothing can start off all by itself. So something incredibly big and fantastically strong must give the Sun a monstrous shove. What it is? This is what I want to know."

"It's a vast puzzle," Butterfly sweetly agreed. "I swear, we will try and be quiet… as best we can…so you can solve this great riddle, just as you've planned. But unfortunately, Tree, and it's not our fault, all kinds of uninvited visitors keep landing on our Leaf."

"Butterfly, I accept your small apology." Then to the Tree's dismay, that boisterous Squirrel with his fat bushy tail landed on a small branch, two green glossy leaves away.

"Hey Tree. What's up?"

"It's not what's up, Squirrel. It's what is down. It's hard to concentrate with so many dangerous Tree Cutters all around."

Squirrel looked down. He studied the ground. "Listen Tree. Listen to me. Don't worry your pretty bark. What isn't here may never come near. Our forest is so big and vast, if those Tree Cutters ever do find you…they'll find you last. And even if they dare to come here…Butterfly will distract them, Spider will frighten them, Mosquito will bite and torment them, and

I will hurl my heaviest nuts down onto their heads and into their hair. So relax your limbs. With a clever pal like me, you have nothing to fear."

"Easy for you to say. But you're not me. You have no idea what it feels like to be a Tree. Go away, Squirrel. Just go away."

Not looking for any kind of squabble, Squirrel took off mumbling, "Who would believe I've been talking to a Tree?"

As a soft wind blew through his sturdy limbs and countless leaves, Tree murmured soundlessly into the wind, "Drat all those noisy creatures who so brazenly live on my leaves. What good is it to be a mighty Tree, if I can't even keep a tiny Spider from crawling all over and tickling me? Am I to have no peace?"

Chapter 14

The Answer

"Hey, Butterfly. You want to play?"

"Nope, Squirrel, I can't. I'm busy."

"You don't look busy to me."

"Well, I am. I am busy looking for answers."

"Answers? Answers? You want answers? You've met the right Squirrel. Ask me anything. When you live on nuts, they sharpen your brain…ask me anything and I will explain."

"You live on nuts? You eat those silly things?"

"Butterfly, a clever old Squirrel once told me…and this is absolutely true…that eating nuts is something even baby Squirrels should do, for nuts not only taste delicious, they are a very hearty food. Just think. If one small nut can grow a great Tree, nuts must be most important to eat."

"Squirrel, if nuts have really sharpened your brain, then you must know the villain who stole all my missing Caterpillar legs."

"You had Caterpillar legs? You're putting me on. I've never ever, in my entire life, seen a Butterfly with Caterpillar legs. And, trust me, I've seen many strange, uncanny things."

"Squirrel, I wasn't a Butterfly when I had my legs. I was a Caterpillar then, you dunderhead."

"Wait. Let me get this straight. You look like a Butterfly. You act like a Butterfly. But you are really a Caterpillar with Wings, not legs. Am I right?"

"Nope. You're wrong. You weren't listening right."

"Are you accusing me of listening wrong?"

"Butterfly, listen! There is an art to burying nuts. You can't bury them too shallow or too deep. Too deep and you'll never find them. Too shallow and the winds and rain will wash them away. I've even been robbed by dastardly dishonest Squirrels. Nothing makes me madder. And worse, I've got so many stashes, sometimes I forget where all my nuts are hidden. Remembering is so much harder than forgetting."

"Look Squirrel. Forget what I said. I've no time to quarrel. You said you have answers. So I'm asking. Where are all my stolen legs? Where have they been hidden?"

"Butterfly, this is a most difficult question. Perhaps they are buried. Like I bury my nuts. This is the wisest way to hide anything of value. I'm assuming your legs had value?"

"Value? Value? They are priceless. Can you can find them for me? Friend to friend?"

"Find them? I'm a Squirrel and a smart one at that. But I can't remember where I bury half my nuts. After a few days my hiding places all look the same. So most of my buried nuts I can't ever claim. Try tossing me an easier question….like who was the villain who stole your legs?

"That's easier? Who cares who stole them. I just want them back. Quick and fast."

"Butterfly. Listen to me. Everybody hides things differently. So we must first decide who would be crazy enough to steal a set of clumsy Caterpillar legs. Once we discover who carried them off, once we know this villain, we can easily deduce just where they are hidden."

"Squirrel. I was sleeping. I sleep with my eyes closed."

"Well let this be a lesson. Next time you nap, keep at least one eye open wide."

"Your advice comes too late. That nap is long over and my legs long missing."

"Your problem, my friend, is a riddle too hard for even a smart Squirrel like me. Without knowing who stole them, there are too many places your legs could be."

"Do you think they are gone forever?"

"It's hard to say. But here's what I'll do. While I'm scrambling for nuts, if I ever see a fancy set of lost Caterpillar legs, I'll bury them deep and carefully mark the place."

"Bury them? They'll get all dirty and be worthless."

"They won't be worthless. You can always polish them up like I polish my nuts…but we're a long way from that. Just remember, if I find them…I promise I'll bring them back. How's that?

"But now I've gotta run. I've lots more trees to climb. More nuts to find." Squirrel left so fast, without even a small wave or tiny farewell, his fancy tail had trouble keeping up.

"Butterfly, that Squirrel's a jerk. He talks through his cheeks." That's all the Mosquito said. The subject was dropped.

Chapter **15**

The Ant Comes Back

Just as the Squirrel took off, the Ant with Amnesia returned. "Why are you back?" An obvious question. But Mosquito asked it anyway.

"Back? Back? Why am I back? Why are you asking me that when I've never been here before?"

"Are you some sort of nut?" Mosquito's eyes grew big. "You were here yesterday…looking for wisdom…wanting to know why we are here? Why we were made? If there is possibly some kind of Grand Plan."

"Impossible. I'm not interested in any Wisdom or Plans. I have a bigger problem now."

"A problem?"

"Can't you tell? It should be obvious. I'm deaf. I can't hear a thing in either ear. And it's quite a big burden to me."

"Deaf? How can you be deaf when you are busy talking to me?"

"I know I can talk. I know I hear words. But I can't hear what I want to hear."

"What can't you hear? You can hear me. And that's what counts."

"Nope. It isn't. I can't hear the important stuff."

"Like what?"

"Like the Sun. Everybody knows the Sun is a burning ball of fire. So it has to go crackle and pop. But I can never hear the Sun coming up. No matter how hard I try. It just silently appears."

"Nobody can hear the Sun come up, you dunderhead."

"Mosquito, I can't hear my own thin body grow, even standing smack in the middle of it. And your enormous Tree. From my place in the Great Ant Line, I've watched it double and triple

"Drat! I'm deaf! But my eyesight is perfect. I'm nowhere near the head of our Great Ant Line. I'm at the rear. Still, I can spot the tastiest scraps and morsels from way back here. I'm really afraid, if they improve my position, and tell me I'm smart enough to march up in front, I won't be able to hear."

in size. But I've never heard a sound. Not a peep. And I know it couldn't grow this tall without making some kind of noise. I must be deaf."

"What if I told you nobody can hear any of these wonders you've just described?"

"I wouldn't believe you. That's what. The whole world can't be deaf."

"Can you hear all that shouting from down below?"

"Of course. That's my friend, Seymore. He's holding my place in the Great Ant Line."

"What's he yelling?"

"That he can't hold the Ant Line forever. And I'd better come quick." Leaning over the edge of the Leaf, the deaf Ant with Amnesia hollered down. "Hold your horses! I hear you! I'm on my way."

Stepping over the edge, the Ant turned back to say, "You guys have been very nice, if not very helpful."

"Watch out for Spider Webs," Butterfly yelled to the Ant with Amnesia on her way down. "I have a bad feeling in my Wings."

"He can't hear you," Mosquito said. "He's deaf."

Chapter 16

Spider Wants A Wife

Mosquito groaned. "Spider! Why in the blazes are you still here? You're legs are messing up our Leaf."

"Y…Ye Gads. I fell back asleep. Dang it! Now I've overslept." Lazily stretching all eight of his legs, Spider opened half an eye and griped. "What t…ti..time is it anyway?"

"It's still several hours 'til dark," Butterfly sighed. "You might as well go back and finish your nap."

"I would go back if I could go back. My dream was so w…wo…wonderful. I was getting m…ma..married to a beautiful Spider bride."

"That was a wasted dream. Dreams are supposed to be fanciful. But not impossible. Spiders don't get married."

"I know. I know. Why do you think this is so?"

"Because," Butterfly patiently explained, "Spiders are way too ugly for true love and romance. That's why. There is no such thing as a gorgeous Spider bride."

"Maybe you're wrong. Maybe there could be a beautiful lady Spider out there, somewhere, just waiting for m…me."

"Your case is hopeless. Even the most attractive lady Spiders are

"Alright. I admit I might be ugly. Maybe very ugly, according to that stuck-up Butterfly. But that's only on the outside. On the inside I'm really quite splendid. I only hope there's a lady Spider somewhere, who can see all the beautiful thoughts and dreams inside of me. It's so unfair. Butterfly is so beautiful. How can she not be having an easy happy life?"

still horrid and homely. The best you could get is a very ugly companion."

"But I want a home. A family. Spiders are denied this joy. It's so unfair! We don't even get to raise our own kids. As soon as they start to grow, they jump off our Webs, traveling away in the wind…anxious to be on their own. I can hear my tiny sons wailing now:

> 'Good-bye Pa! We're off on the very next breeze. With luck we won't break any legs or crack our k…kn… knees. But we have to leave. Because long ago it was decreed the world must have a Spider under every rock and in every tree. So Good-bye Pa! You've taught us all we need to know to catch our victims so we can grow. But, Pa, we wish, we wish we didn't have to go.'

"Now, Spider, don't go getting all sloppy and soppy." Butterfly spread out her lovely Wings. "If you had lots of baby Spiders to raise, you would have to share your Web. They'd be running up and down all over the place. Smashing it to pieces. Besides, there's a big important Spider Rule you would be breaking."

"I would? What's that?"

"It's one Spider to every Web. Spiders are too horrid to be social…to share a Web…to build it together…repair it together…suck disgusting blood from their victims together."

"If you're right, I'm doomed to live a lonely miserable life." Spider dropped his monstrous head. He kept it low. "You're sure nothing can be done?"

"Nothing. All you can do, Spider, is think about something else. Distract yourself. Make your mind forget you are going to be down in the dumps and miserable forever."

"Distract myself? Forget? Forget I am doomed to misery? That's i…im…impossible!"

"It's hard. But it can be done. First, Spider, you must completely empty your head. Toss out all those thoughts of the miserable, empty, gloomy, lonely, loveless life awaiting you ahead. Now you can fill your empty head with glorious, all new thoughts. Distracting thoughts."

"Butterfly, I'm trying. But it's impossible to think of anything else but my miserable, empty, gloomy, lonely, loveless life ahead."

"You must try harder. For starters, look at me squarely and put all your attention to answering this distracting difficult question."

"Ask me anything. I'm very smart. Cleverly smart."

"And you're very agile too. Which brings me to my question. How can you Spiders so easily and quickly run up and down your sticky Webs, when any other creature that touches it, sticks tight. It cannot move. How is this so? What ancient secret keep you from getting stuck?"

Spider took one of his favorite legs and scratched his massive head. "Beats me. I was b...bo...born with this talent. I have other amazing talents too."

"Other talents? You look quite horrid and talentless to me. A homely creature is all I see."

"Nope. There's more to me. Once a visitor hits my Web, I know precisely how to tie it up, numb it with my special spider spit, then sit back and wait a bit. That's all there is to proper Spider etiquette. I could teach you how a Spider dines by sipping blood..if you really want to learn. It isn't hard."

"You're very kind... but I think I'll pass."

"But Butterfly, teaching you these skills, sharing a meal, will definitely distract me. You'll love my bloody moth stew."

"Thanks, but no thanks, Spider. There is a great deal of difference between sipping the pure nectar of flowers and slurping up yucky blood."

"Blood is better. Quite delicious in fact. But then again, I don't have a sweet tooth. Actually, neither of us have any teeth." Spider paused to laugh at his wit, then continued on. "Perhaps we have more in common than you think."

"Spider. We have nothing in common. I was only trying to distract you from your melancholy thoughts. But I can see you're not so easily distracted."

"You're so wrong, Butterfly. I'm all distracted now. I've totally forgotten my m…mi…miserable, gloomy, friendless, desperate lonely life. Until it's time to spin my dinner Web tonight, I'm sitting right here. With you. Distracting myself. Thinking up new clever ways to find myself a beautiful Spider wife."

"Did you hear nothing I said?"

"I heard every word you said. But others say m…mm…miracles can happen…that sometimes d…dreams really do come true."

"Spider, your mind is a mess. I must confess there is no helping you. I'm out of here. I'm gone."

Chapter 17

Evolution

Spider's unhappiness rubbed off on Butterfly. "You know, Mosquito, I'm really missing my feet. I still can't believe they were stolen away. Every single one. Why did such a bad thing happen to such a good Caterpillar like me?"

"Butterfly, I'm beginning to suspect your feet weren't lost. Or stolen. Have you not heard of Evolution? How creatures change slowly over time?"

"Of course I've heard of Evolution. Do I look dumb? But what has Evolution to do with me? Evolution takes a billion years to make one teeny tiny change. And I don't think I have lived that long. I'm guessing I'm not so very old."

"Then I will explain. In your case, Butterfly, when you fell asleep inside your tight cocoon, Evolution changed its pace from very slow to very fast. To have lost your legs so quickly, and gained two splendid Wings, is Evolution at its best. You should be extra happy."

"Happy? I'm tired of lugging these gigantic Wings around. I want to go back and be a little green Caterpillar again…but I can't be a Caterpillar again until I find my missing legs. And not even one tiny foot remains."

"So let us be practical Butterfly. Scientific. Exactly how many did you lose? Precisely how many legs are missing?"

"Mosquito, that's one of my problems. I'm not sure just how many legs I had. I was always so busy climbing vines and chewing leaves, I never thought to count them."

"But you do know how to count?"

"Actually, I'm not too good at it."

"Can you at least remember, then, if you had more legs or less legs than our ugly Spider has?"

"I'm afraid my memory is a bit vague. And you've asked a very hard question. If my memory is correct, my legs never went in a circle."

"Circle or straight doesn't matter. Now think hard, Butterfly. Either you had more legs or less legs. Our Spider has eight. So…did you have seven or nine?"

"I have no idea. I'm not too good at adding. I seem to be a bit slow at any kind of counting."

"You know, Butterfly, you've set me to thinking. Maybe knowing how to add isn't all that important. Let's start our search by doing some serious subtracting. We must figure out how many feet got subtracted in that tight cocoon you were stupid enough to spin. Then, if we reverse our thinking, and quickly add up all the legs that got subtracted, we will know how many legs you started with. This is very simple math."

"I hope my little feet aren't sitting somewhere. All broken to bits and pieces."

"I have no idea, Butterfly. I'm not even certain if we should be searching for Butterfly legs that went missing, or Caterpillar legs that are lost. I suspect your tiny mind is not up to a logic problem such as this.

"Then again," Mosquito added, "in a case of serious counting stupidity, such as you obviously have, perhaps it is best to give up both adding and subtracting, and try and solve something of no importance at all. This is always so much easier. This is what the whole world does."

"I'm sitting here, trying not to think. But I think...trying not to think is even harder than thinking. Because as hard as I try not to think, if I close my eyes, I still see all my missing little Caterpillar feet."

"You mean you want me to think of something not important? To give up higher math?"

"It is for the best, Butterfly. You will find yourself far happier this way. Serious thinking is work. Hard work. This is why the biggest questions…like why you got huge impressive Wings and I got stuck with these ratty things…remain riddles. It's exhausting to think too hard. Nobody wants to do it. Nobody has time.

"Which is precisely why, Butterfly, the world is filled with unimportant thoughts. But nobody calls them unimportant thoughts. We call this type of shallow thinking 'rest and relaxation'. You must now forget your missing legs…stop wondering if you are a Caterpillar or Butterfly…and make your mind do easy thinking. You will be so much happier this way. Do you get me Butterfly?"

"Gotcha. I think. So maybe I should try not to think at all?"

"You're on your way to happiness, Butterfly. You're on your way."

Chapter 18

Two Big Eyes

"Butterfly, what are you staring at?"

"Mosquito, don't move. There's a giant feathered creature observing our Leaf. With the biggest circle eyes I've ever seen. And each of these eyes is twice my size."

"Did you ask him who he is?"

"Of course I did. He swears he's an Owl, whatever it is an Owl is."

"We must be brave, Butterfly."

"I'm trying Mosquito…but he looks awfully big and mean to me."

"Stay calm. Let us not do anything rash. Just casually ask how he got here without making any noise."

The Great Owl easily overheard. "Owls never make noise. It's impossible to hear me come. Impossible to hear me go. In fact, I can't stand noise. Which is why I can't sleep with all the commotion coming from this particular Leaf. And when I cannot sleep, I cannot think. And an Owl must think in order to be wise."

"What makes you think you are so wise?"

THE WISE OWL...THINKING

"The other Owls constantly tell me so. This is how I know. Owls never lie."

"There are other Owls with big circle eyes? You're not the only one?"

"Of course I'm not the only one. There are other Owls just like me."

Butterfly stayed skeptical. "Owl, just where are you from?"

"From the top of our Tree."

"Our Tree? You live in my Tree?"

"It's not your Tree. It's mine. And this constant shouting has got to stop! All your noise floats straight to the top."

Butterfly lost interest in the Owl's big eyes. She was staring now at the Owl's great feet. Too huge to fit on any leaf.

"Oh my. You do have quite enormous feet."

"Enormous but not ordinary. I can use my feet as hands when I want to eat."

"You're kidding me."

"Great Owls don't kid. Great Owls don't joke. And Owls hate noise when they are trying to think."

"Owl, long ago, I myself had lots of feet. Far more than you. Many more than two. I used them to walk and to hike and to climb. But never to eat. What else can Owls do?"

"What else can I do? What else can I do? Have you any idea what a wise genius you are talking to? When I'm in the mood, I can turn my head almost all the way around...not just from side to side like you." And the Wise Owl twisted his head in a circle so wide, his eyes could see almost everything going on behind.

"Now show me," the Wise Owl said, as his eyes were once again facing straight ahead, "what Butterflies can do?"

"I have no talents. I have no skills. All I have are these two fabulous Butterfly wings."

"What a pity. Because beauty must always fade. Your wings won't always be as beautiful as they are today. But my invisible wisdom (for which I'm known) will only grow sharper as I grow old."

"Now I want more than ever," Butterfly cried, "to become a Caterpillar once again. Do you think it is possible, with your great big eyes, you can find all those little lost legs of mine?"

"What do they look like?"

"They are quite splendid. Mostly green and a little on the plump side as I recall. A perfect Caterpillar size."

"The Great Owl then wisely asked, "How many legs did you have? How many have you lost?"

"Unfortunately, I cannot add. I cannot subtract. Apparently, I do not have a head for math."

Unfazed, the Wise Owl twisted his head around so he could see the entire ground, both in front of their Tree and way behind. His brilliant eyes searched everywhere those tiny legs could be.

He did all this while his feathers made not even a tiny sound. Finally he said in a voice low and deep, "Butterfly, I have bad news for you. Your legs are nowhere to be found. They are simply not anywhere around."

"Maybe you could look some more?"

"My eyes are huge. My mind is wise. It's an insult to ask an Owl to do anything twice. But I will give you, for free, some very wise and lofty Owl advice. 'Don't think of your loss. Just think of your gain. Your feet may be gone, but your wings remain.'

"Now I must be off. I've more wondrous thoughts to think. And when I get back to the top of our Tree…I don't want to hear any more noise coming from this busy Leaf. Because I will get mad. And when I get mad I behave very bad. It's a temper problem all wise Owl's have."

"Look closely! You are staring at both my hands and my feet…feet when I want to stand and think…hands when I'm starving and need to eat."

He said this as he stared at his two clever feet that were also his hands when he wanted to eat. Then silently he spread his wings. Butterfly and Mosquito watched in awe as the Owl with the big circle eyes flew quietly, silently, back up to the top, to that awesome point where their Tree finally stopped.

"Mosquito, he seems civilized…but why do I have a bad feeling in my Wings?"

"Butterfly, those Wings of yours are foolish things. Don't you know we each wander paths filled with many twists and turns. But if we go carefully, slowly, looking both this way and that, there is an excellent chance we can avoid the worst paths as we search our way toward happiness.

"You know what else I'm thinking Butterfly? I'm thinking you really should toss away those dratted Wings and find some other way to fly."

Chapter 19

An Owl For Dinner

Spider snapped up from his second nap, just as the Great Owl flew silently quietly past. "Ye gads, Butterfly, what was that?"

"That, my dear Spider, was an Owl. Or so he said. You slept through his most interesting visit."

"Owl or not, that was some set of feathers he had. They might be quite light and delicious to eat. I'm gonna trap him in my very next Web. I'm already hungry."

"You can't be serious? Did you see his eyes? He can see everything! Which is one of the reasons he is so wise. By twisting his head practically all the way around, he can see what is clearly in front of him and what's hidden way behind. He is far too clever to be caught in any Web you weave."

"Maybe yes. Maybe no. And I'm thinking 'yes' just might be so. Where does he live, do you suppose?"

"You're in luck. He lives at the very top of our Tree. But you have a long steep cold climb if you want Owl meat or Owl feathers to eat."

The Spider lifted his big circle head up high, at least as far as it could rise, trying to figure exactly how fast he would have to climb. He took his time deciding just how tasty a meal of Owl might be.

"I'll give it a g..go..go." And moving all of his legs with incredible speed, jumped off their Leaf and headed straight up into the bright blue sky.

Spider was gone for a very long time...returning from his trip with a shabby body and cranky mind.

"Good heavens! What happened to you? You look all bushed. You look all beat. I'm assuming you didn't find any Owl feathers or meat to eat?"

"Butterfly, I started my climb in great circular shape. But there are tiny r...re..red ants all over this Tree. It was impossible to keep them from biting me.

"But I didn't give up. As soon as I passed those horrible ants, a cold wind blew by and I almost died. All of me grew cold and numb. I could hardly feel my frozen legs, each with its very own brilliant brain.

"But I didn't give up. When a giant cloud settled on the top of our Tree, I was in grave danger because this grey cloud of fog surrounded me. And I couldn't see.

"But I didn't give up. I didn't stop until I finally arrived at the very top. And let me tell you, this Earth is a sight to behold when you are up so high. It's not flat at all, but is fat

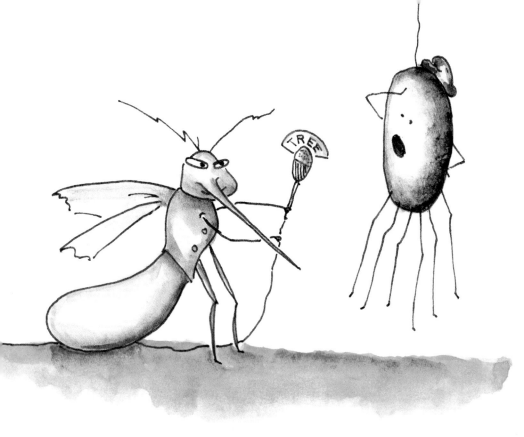

"Oh woe is me. What a bitter trip it turned out to be. Biting ants. Blinding clouds. Freezing winds. Scattered leaves. Frost bite in all my legs. I watched them turn from black to grey. But finally, I stood at the top of our Tree. I looked around…and blast it all…that dratted Owl couldn't be found. He was nowhere around. There was nothing to do, but head back down. So that's it, Mosquito. I'm trying to recover now. I feel faint."

and round, just like this tummy I carry with me. Obviously, 'round' is the best way to be."

"Did you happen to see, from your great vantage point, any little green legs that once belonged to me?"

"Butterfly, I had far more important things to do…glorious scenes to view. Rivers and lakes and trees. That kind of stuff.

I was so engrossed as I stood smack on that dazzling pointy top, I caught myself just as I was about to tumble off."

"Then what did you do?"

"What did I do? What did I do? I spun a giant, silken, glorious Web, you nincompoop, just like I said I would do. I never lie."

"So what happened then? Why are you back so soon?"

"Because that dratted Owl was no where to be found! Nothing landed in my Web. Nothing at all. Not a moth. Not a fly. Not one Owl feather could I find! And after all the hard work I went to, too."

"So what did you do?"

"What did I do? What did I do? I turned myself right around and climbed all the way, passed those dratted ants, back down. So here I am. This is all that's left of me. I'm tired. I'm hungry. I've had nothing to eat. And I'm disappointed too. Now I'll never taste Owl feathers or sample Owl stew."

The defeated Spider slumped. "I guess before I get some sleep, I'd better spin a quick Web and catch me an ordinary tasteless moth to eat. I'm starving."

"Just don't spin your sticky Web anywhere I'm near! Don't you dare spin it here!"

"Butterfly, I never spin Webs where I'm going to sleep."

"Ye Gads! You can't sleep here! I just cleaned up this Leaf. You left it a mess!"

"Butterfly, get used to me. This Leaf is big enough for three. I'm starting to like not only you…I'm beginning to like that snotty Mosquito too."

Butterfly slumped. "I never thought gaining a friend could be such unhappy news."

Chapter 20

The Ant With Amnesia

The Ant with Amnesia was back. "Hey! Guys! Anybody home?"

"Hey…Ant. It's great to see you back."

"Mosquito, I've never been here before in my life! But your mistake is alright. Most of us Ants all look alike."

"Have you no memories at all in your head?"

"All my memories have fled. I have Amnesia instead. I can't remember one tiny thing. I'm told I have an empty head. So, Mosquito, I have a big favor I need you to do. I've heard you are very smart. And I need some facts, fast, to put in my brain. Even if they won't remain."

"Let me get this straight. You need some facts, fast, to put in your head. Am I right?"

"Just one big important fact will do."

The Mosquito rubbed his ratty wings. "Ant, it's your lucky day. I am willing to give you a fact. Would you like it to be big and round or small and square?"

The Ant tried to think with its empty head. And finally said, "I don't care. But I want it to be true."

"OK my friend. Here is your fact. ONE AND ONE MAKE TWO."

"This sounds indeed like a very big fact. But how am I to carry it back?"

"In your head, you dope."

"Well, it would be a lot easier if you could put it on my back. It's way too big and way too heavy to carry inside my head. I'll lose it."

"I feel like there's something on my back…but I can't think what it could be. And why would I have anything on my back? I must be imagining things."

"Ant, even the biggest fact should fit in your head. Especially since your head is obviously empty. There's got to be lots of room."

"I've got plenty of empty space. I agree with you. But I must have a hole in it somewhere. Because as soon as a fact goes in, it disappears. I look and it isn't there. It isn't anywhere."

"That's not Amnesia. That's Stupidity. But if you turn yourself around, I'll tie this fact carefully on your back. But don't let it break in two. If you drop this fact, it will break in half. Then each half can only add up to ONE.

Each half can never add up to TWO. You will have a fact that isn't true."

Mosquito smiled as he waved the Ant off. But he didn't have much hope. "That Ant's mind is all scrambled. Poor thing. Butterfly, I'll bet you a million Spiders that Ant has already forgotten he's carrying a big important fact on his back. But I guess there is nothing, nothing more that we can do."

Chapter **21**

Spider Gets A Tail

Spider was sitting quietly. Totally still. Doing nothing much. Just waiting for Squirrel. "So, Mosquito, where is he already? How many nuts can one Squirrel bury?"

"He'll come when he's ready. Not when you're ready for him to come. That's how Squirrels work. What's the big hurry, Spider, anyway?"

"Mosquito, I've decided I need a tail. A big bushy tail. Just like Squirrel's. And I need it fast."

"Why would a horrid Spider like you want a tail? You're already tripping over eight ugly legs. Where would you put a big bushy tail, anyway?"

"I'll find room. Trust me. Even if I have to m…mo…move around a leg or two."

"Trust what? Trust who?" The Squirrel arrived just ahead of his fanciful tail. Curious as usual.

"Look Squirrel. I need a little favor. I need a b..bi..big bushy tail."

"Why would you, a dull repulsive Spider, want a big glorious tail like mine?"

"Precisely because I am ugly. Everyone tells me so. But a lavish tail will enhance my looks. Make me less scary. Then maybe I could get some friends. I really want a hundred friends. But I guess one friend will do."

"That's impossible. Spiders are born too grotesque for friends. That's life. Some of us are lucky. Some aren't. But if it's a tail you want, you'll have to see the White Hen at the bottom of our Tree. When she is not busy laying eggs...rumor has it she is great at growing tails."

"I'm off!"

"Wait! There's more. You've got to turn left at the base of our Tree, past six low bushes and six tall trees. You'll find the White Hen roosting there."

"I'm off!" Spider said again.

* * * *

"Hey! Hen!"

"Who's there. Who keeps calling me?"

"It's me. Over here."

The White Hen looked this way and that, almost stepping on a black Spider that was too ugly to even eat. "Yuk! Get away! What do you want? Why are you bothering me? I'm too busy to waste my time talking to a ghastly Spider like you. I've got eggs to lay and other important chores to do."

"Hen! Wait! P…pl..please! Don't go! Your friend, the Squirrel, said you could help me grow a most fabulous tail."

"What kind do you want? What tail do you have in mind?"

"I want it big and b…bu…bushy. Just like Squirrel's. Is it hard to do? How does this sound?"

"It sounds stupid. That's how it sounds. How impractical can you be? But it doesn't matter what you want. Because I can give you a tail, but I can't ever predict just what it will be. Take it or leave it."

"I swear! I'm not a picky eater. I eat everything. Termites…when I can find them. I love, I really love, flying ants. But I couldn't bring myself to gobble up that Spider. Yuk! So I gave him his tail… because he didn't ask for my advice. He just asked for a tail. Now if he had asked for my advice, I would have told him a tail is the last thing he needs. His problem is too many legs."

"This stick doesn't look very big. But let me tell you…it's heavy. I couldn't lift it if I didn't have these eight amazing legs. Even though, because of them I get picked on and ridiculed too. I'm hoping a tail, which Hen swears is hidden in the green gooey stuff she stuck on this stick, will do the trick."

"I'll take it. That's what I'll do. But if it's a long thin mouse tail, I'm going to be very mad at you."

The White Hen was too busy to listen. "Here," she said, carefully handing Spider a stick with green gooey stuff all over it. "Rub this on the spot exactly where you want your tail to be…and come back in seven days…come sun or wind or rain. I need to make sure it's growing straight."

Spider returned to his Leaf on the tree. It was a very slow and dismal trip. He had to use his two fastest legs to carry Hen's green gooey stick, being careful not to trip or slip.

"What's that green mess you're holding there?" Squirrel was already holding his nose. "It smells terrible!"

"It's for my tail. But I need you to help me rub it on. Your friend the White Hen said a decent tail takes seven days."

Still holding his nose, Squirrel cautiously took the smelly stick. "So where do you want this tail? Between which legs?"

"I want it in the rear. So it will follow me closely, just like yours. Besides, I've never seen a tail that leads."

"I suppose then, since you are made in a circle, unlike me, I had better first find your eyes, then rub this stick on the opposite side."

Spider hurriedly twisted around, but his legs got all tangled, and he bumped into Squirrel, knocking the stick with the green gooey stuff out of Squirrel's hands and it hit the ground.

"There goes my tail. What rotten luck."

Squirrel peered over the edge of the Leaf, and saw the stick with the green gooey stuff covered in dust and dirt. "So what kind of tail do you think you lost?"

"I don't have the slightest idea. That stuck-up Hen wouldn't say. She wouldn't predict. All she did was hand me this green gooey stick. Then she cackled and walked away."

"You mean you took a tail, sight unseen? That's the most stupid thing you could have done. You're lucky I dropped that stick."

"That's easy for you to say. You've got a tail that's bigger than you and most impressive too."

"Would it make you feel any better if I told you that even with a fabulous tail like mine, the rest of you would still be a horrid disgusting Spider? You can't exactly hide an ugly fat body and eight ghastly legs... even if there is the slim possibility those legs all have individual brains. Does this comfort you a bit?"

"Not a bit," Spider tearfully said. "Not a smidgen. I've had better days."

Chapter 22

Heads Or Tails

As soon as Spider disappeared with his green gooey stick, a gorgeous Brown Rooster caught up with Hen. "So what kind of tail did you give him? I'm curious."

"I told him I couldn't be sure. That he'd have to wait and see."

"But you must have a hunch. You're a very clever Hen."

"I got into tail making by accident. I had planned to spend my life just laying eggs. But as I was pecking near the barn one day, I came across a pail and several sticks. The pail was filled with this green gooey stuff, and when I dipped in a stick, to my amazement, out came a long thin tail. So I kept dipping in various sticks and out came different tails. But gradually I ran out of sticks. Then I ran out of stuff. Which is why I only make tails when I can find both the right sticks and right stuff. This is why I can't alway predict. I'm never sure which tail will come from which stick."

"Well, Rooster, there's not much anyone can do for such a distasteful creature, what with eight grotesque legs sticking out every which way. His circle was already full. The only kind of tail I could possibly fit in was a thin stringy rat-like thing."

"Will it stick up in the air, or drag on the ground as some rat tails are prone to do?"

"I can't be certain. I can't be sure. To be honest, I can't stand spiders, and I just wanted him to take his eight legs and go away…not hang around upsetting my day. He is always going to look frightful."

"I think he'll be back."

"And why is that?"

"Because I was scratching the ground, at the base of his Tree, and a green gooey stick landed very close, too close, to me."

"So what does this mean?"

"It means that clumsy Spider dropped your stick. And has probably already ordered his eight brilliant legs, each of which he swears has an extra brain, to bring him back…and fast."

"Yuk! I'm going away. I'm not going to deal with that vain Spider any more today. He is yours to deal with Rooster. Tell him what you may."

Chapter **23**

The Brown Rooster

"Hey Rooster? Where's the White Hen?

"She's gone."

"Gone? Gone?" Spider was aghast. "So when is she coming back?"

"It's hard to say."

"But I've got to see her. I've l…lo..lost my tail."

"How can you lose a tail you've never had?"

"I didn't exactly lose my tail. I lost my green gooey stick. And I need a new one. Quick."

"You're out of luck. Even if she comes back, it's one per customer, per day. That's it."

"You mean I can't get another tail?"

"Nope. I mean you can't get another green gooey stick. She doesn't make them very often, anyway."

"My life is ruined. I'm lost."

"Lost? You're not lost. You're right here in front of me. I can see you clearly."

"Numbskull. Not that kind of lost. Oh never mind. You wouldn't understand."

"Spider, you probably wouldn't have liked your tail any way. A thin rat-like tail would have constantly got caught between all your various legs. And with a big fat bushy tail, you'd be tripping and falling all over the place."

"You don't understand. Now I'll never be beautiful. I'll be ugly my whole life." Tears came to Spider's eyes. It's probably the first time a lowly Spider has ever cried.

"What makes you think you're ugly?"

"All spiders are ugly. Everyone has told me so. Butterfly swears I'm even too ugly to find a bride."

"Well. She's not all wrong. But she's not all right either. Another ghastly spider might find you rather attractive."

"Do you think so?"

"Well I can't be certain…but I know if you grew a tail, you would scare most lady spiders off. They are all madly looking for ugly male spiders with exactly eight ugly legs. Assuming they can count. Adding a tail would be a big mistake."

"So you think I'm better off without one?"

"Actually, I think you're better off without a bride…but that's a problem for another day. Let me just say, to be practical,

"Spider. Why be glum. Look at your miserable life this way. You are already as ugly as you can possibly get. You can never get any uglier. That would be impossible. Which means you can only improve. So you must rejoice. Be merry. Be happy. But don't consider this a bit of free advice. Consider that I am sharing with you an obvious scientific fact."

a tail could only get in your way. Is it so very hard to be happy just the way you are made?"

"Yes. I'm tired of being me. I want to be somebody else."

"Impossible. Everybody else is already taken."

"Maybe I could work a trade."

"I don't think anyone, from a Centipede to a Toad, would grab at a chance to become a Spider."

"So what am I to do?"

"Spider, I can give you some fine advice. And I will tell you first it is free. Which means you won't follow it. I've learned anything that's free, is never much appreciated. In fact, it isn't appreciated at all."

"I'll appreciate it. I promise. Just tell me already."

"OK. Here goes. 'Your only hope is to be the very best Spider you can possibly be. Remember, Spiders rid the world of many terrible things. Be proud of who you are. Forget about beauty. Beauty fades. But goodness and kindness never go away. They grow stronger everyday.'"

"That's the most stupid advice I've ever heard. I'm glad it was free. I wouldn't pay a penny for it."

As he ambled off, the Brown Rooster heard him say, "Goodness? Kindness? What a wasted day."

Chapter **24**

What Can I Do?

"Butterfly. Why so droopy? I myself am in a happy hungry hunting mood."

"Mosquito, don't bother me with food. Not now. I'm too confused. I still can't decide if I'm a Caterpillar or a Butterfly. What do you think? Be honest. Which do you suppose I really am?"

"You're asking me? Your recent enemy?

"Mosquito, in spite of your distasteful ways, and disgusting need to guzzle blood, I have nobody else to ask. I've been carrying this puzzle inside me for too long a time. It's getting too big for me to continue to hide."

"So spill it already."

"I already spilled it! I've been telling you forever how unhappy I am with the way I've been made. I'm asking you what do you think I should do? I'm all confused."

The Mosquito affected a most scholarly pose. Proboscis ahead. Tattered wings opposed. "Butterfly, be more specific about your complaint. Is it your outside or your inside that you want to change?"

"It's both, you idiot. It's both. I just don't know who I am.

"First I thought Mosquito was a jerk. Then I revised
my opinion, and decided he was worse. But as I got
to know him, I've come to see he's much smarter
than that stupid looking proboscis of his led me to
believe. I've come to see he might be even a touch
bit smarter than me...but just a tiny touch."

Some days I think I am still meant to be a Caterpillar, but then, I decide I would miss being a Butterfly. Everyday I get more confused. I just don't know which way I was made. My dear Mosquito, are you smart enough to figure out what I'm trying to say?"

"Of course I'm smart. Do I look stupid? So…Butterfly, let's just suppose you found your Caterpillar legs."

"Mosquito, it's so much more than all my missing legs. Everybody else seems so happy and satisfied with the way they are made."

"That's nonsense, Butterfly. Nobody is entirely pleased. If our Spider is so content, why is he running around trying to find a bushy tail when he already has too many legs?"

"Mosquito, Spider only wants a tail like Squirrel to fancy up his outside. Believe it or not, he is quite happy to be a horrid Spider on the inside. So he can't possibly be as unhappy as me. I'm so mixed up. Nobody will tell me what I'm supposed to be."

"Don't panic little Butterfly. I have a plan."

"And why should I trust your plan?

"Butterfly, when you must constantly land on human feet and human hands, each landing requires a complex set of devious plans."

"I'm listening, Mosquito. I'm listening."

"All right Butterfly. Here's how you must proceed. Do you know how to imaginate?"

"Of course I do. Everybody does. I've probably got a bigger brighter imagination than you."

"Good. So on Day One, you must imagine you are a Caterpillar. And you must do this every minute for one whole day. It's won't be easy. You cannot use your Wings. Not once. And instead of sipping nectar, you must try and chew some leaves. But not this Leaf!"

"Mosquito, your Plan doesn't sound so hard."

"Butterfly, you are still only halfway done. On Day Two, you must now practice being a Butterfly. From dawn to dark, you must think like a Butterfly. And act like one. And I must tell you…real pretending can be very hard. It isn't something easily done."

"Mosquito, don't worry about me. I'm use to pretending. My imagination is a very big part of me."

"Good. Because now my Plan gets harder yet. On Day Three you must carefully review both Day One and Day Two. Ask yourself if you were most happy as a Caterpillar or as a

"I hope Butterfly decides to be a Caterpillar like me. We are such lucky things. The only work we have to do is once, just once, spin a teeny tiny silk cocoon. Other than that, all we do is nibble and eat. In fact, as soon as I'm finished up here, I'm going to slowly mosey over and snack upon their glossy Leaf! Give my-self a special treat."

Butterfly. Once your decision is made, your friends will accept whichever..whoever...whatever...it is you decide you truly are."

"What if they don't?"

Mosquito remained in his scholarly pose. "It's probably true, some friends may drift away. But I'm sure those who deeply love you will stick around and stay."

"What if everybody laughs at me?"

"Ignore them! They are probably jealous...because you get to choose who you want to be. Not everybody gets to have such a big important role in their own private destiny. Most creatures never question who they are...and what they are... and why they came to be.

"But remember, and don't ever forget, just because you are born one way, doesn't mean you cannot change. You are who you 'know' you are. All you gotta do is listen to your intuition, little Butterfly. Intuitionate!"

"You know what I'm thinking, Mosquito. I'm thinking we could become the best of companions. If only you didn't love to slurp up blood. Is that something you might change?"

"Give up my blood? What else would I eat? How dumb can you be? Butterfly, if I didn't love you so much I'd toss you off our Leaf."

"Does that mean we're friends?"

"We're friends, Butterfly. We're friends."

"Forever?"

"Forever, my friend. Whatever it is you decide you are."

Chapter **25**

Butterfly Meets The White Hen

Staring out over the edge of her Leaf, Butterfly sat mumbling to herself, and to anybody else who wanted to hear mumbling. "Maybe, just maybe, that stupid Mosquito's not totally stupid. Maybe he's just part-way stupid. Perhaps I'll follow his crazy advice and pretend I'm a Caterpillar again. But...no way can I use these spindly Butterfly legs. They're worthless."

"So what's up? What thoughts are circling in that mixed-up Butterfly brain?"

"Mosquito, I've decided to test your crazy idea...and pretend I'm a Caterpillar again. But I can't even pretend without some decent feet. So I'm off to see the White Hen. To get myself some sturdy legs so I can start your plan."

"Save yourself a trip, Butterfly. The White Hen doesn't do legs. Just tails."

"Well I'm going to see her anyway. She may change her mind. I can be very persuasive you know."

"Believe me. I know. So...are you going to walk out over the edge of our Leaf and down our Tree, like real Caterpillars do?"

"Don't be a jerk, Mosquito. It would take me all night and most of tomorrow with these skimpy legs. I'll have to fly. I'll have to use my Wings."

"Just remember, Butterfly, when you get to the base of our Tree, fly high. You have to pass six short bushes with bright red berries, then six tall trees."

Being smart, Butterfly didn't lose her way. "Good day to you, my dear bonny Hen."

The White Hen looked up to see a gorgeous orange Butterfly.

"Lovely Hen. I've been told you are the most clever, most brilliant Hen alive…and I desperately need one of your green gooey sticks to grow some legs…if it's not too much trouble, of course."

"How many sticks do you want, dearie? One stick can only make one leg. So tell me precisely how many sticks you need. I haven't got all day."

"Hen, I'm not exactly certain. I'm not too good at either adding or subtracting. You wouldn't by any chance know how many legs little green Caterpillars usually have?"

"I don't study Caterpillars, dearie. I eat them. I gobble them up. Caterpillars are soft and delicious. Then again, anything green is usually tasty."

Frightened now that Hen might guess her Caterpillar past, Butterfly was deciding to take off as fast as she could fly, when that crazy Poet Snake came slithering up. Mad! Boiling mad! Rattles rattling!

"Bless my feathers. That rude Butterfly flew off before I could tell her I'm no magician. Whatever comes out of my green gooey stick is almost impossible to predict. Still, after studying that sassy Snake, with his crummy rhymes and verses, I was tempted to create for her, instead of a set of ordinary Caterpillar feet, a glorious tail with genuine rattles. Who knows? She might be back. What hasn't happened yet can always come to be. The future is always stuffed with more feathers and more possibilities."

"You bloody Butterfly! You used your Wings to cut in line! I got here first. I want legs too!! And I need them far worse than you!"

"You're just a miserable Snake? Why would you want legs?"

"Why? Why? Because I can't get any respect crawling on the ground. I'm a brilliant Poet, if I say so myself. And I want to walk. And run. And skip. I want to be important."

"Snake, it's not difficult to be important. It's no big deal. It's all in your attitude. All in your brain. But skipping is very difficult. I once had legs and could walk and run. But skipping was out of the question."

"So I won't skip. But I got here first."

"Will you two stop squabbling! Might I point out something both you imbeciles have obviously missed. My specialty is tails. I make glorious tails. I only make legs by accident…when something goes dreadfully wrong."

"But I don't need a tail. I've already got a fancy one." Twisting and slithering about, the Poet Snake proudly displayed not only his tail, but his fabulous collection of rattles. From biggest to littlest.

"Bless my feathers. That is an excellent tail!" Hen seemed truly amazed. "I've never figured out how to do a tail with rattles. You're quite a lucky Snake."

"I'm not lucky. I'm miserable. The minute I show off my rattles, everybody runs off. Nobody's impressed.

"You? Miserable? At least you know you are a Snake. I'm not even certain if I'm a Caterpillar or a Butterfly."

"You mean you can't make up your mind just what you are?

That's absurd! You're obviously a Butterfly. I knew that the minute I slithered up."

"Snake, we are not always what we seem. A Caterpillar's soul lives inside of me, even though a Butterfly is what you see. I look one way but feel another. My outside and my inside somehow got mismatched during a long and most unusual nap… but I won't go into that."

"You're talking gibberish. How can you be other than the Butterfly I see? I shall compose a new poem. I shall call it 'Ode To Stupidity'. The Poet began to sing. "Once I met a Butterfly…who knew how to fly but was stupid inside…"

"Just shut up! You are only a Snake. A simple slithering Snake. You could never understand my longing to be something other than what I am…other than what you see. It's true, I'm uncertain whether a Caterpillar or Butterfly is what I was meant to be. But my confusion isn't stupid. It's a great catastrophe not to like the way you are made, not to be what others see."

Getting impatient, Hen interrupted. "Stop rambling, Butterfly. I haven't got all day. Do you want a tail or not?"

Butterfly looked at Hen's jabbering beak. It seemed to be coming closer and closer. Maybe a bit too close.

"No, Hen. I just decided I don't want a tail. And I don't want any legs today either." Without any kind of good-by or farewell, Butterfly took off as fast as she could fly, whirling high, skimming fast back over the six bushes with red berries and six tall trees.

The White Hen, watching Butterfly so quickly disappear, was somewhat impressed. But not dazzled. "Good riddance, I say. I didn't have time to do any tails or legs today, anyway."

"You won't reconsider?" asked a very unhappy Snake.

"Snake, even if I could give you four shiny new legs, you would still be nothing more than a common Lizard. And I can't think of a single thing good about lizards."

The Poet Snake groaned. "So I guess I'm stuck with being a Snake. Then I'll say good day to you Hen, even though it isn't a good day at all. It's a blasted miserable day."

"Good day to you Snake. And Snake, if you want a clever Hen's opinion…I think you're very smart to stick to slithering. But you might want to give up on the poetry. There must be something much more useful a Snake with so many wondrous rattles can do…although nothing comes to mind."

Chapter 26

No Legs Today

"So how did it go?"

"Not so good, Mosquito. Not so good. Why didn't you tell me that stuck-up Hen is insultingly rude. And her specialty isn't even legs. Did you know she only does legs by accident? Only if something goes dreadfully wrong and her gooey stick turns pink, not green…something she swears she can never predict.

"Worse, she eats Caterpillars, you know. She told me so. She gobbles them up. And I could tell from the way her beady eyes were following me, she was ready to gobble me up too. I think she could see there was lots of Caterpillar still inside of me.

"And then it hit me, Mosquito. I was suddenly gloriously happy I was a Butterfly and could fly off and not get eaten to pieces by that cunning Hen. Caterpillars are helpless, you know. Their legs can only run slow. Poor things.

"So that's when I knew, Mosquito. That's when I finally understood. I have the soul of a Caterpillar tucked tight inside this beautiful body of a Butterfly. So I am both, Mosquito. I am both. Now…I'm trying to decide if I should call myself a 'Butterpillar' or maybe a 'Caterfly'. What do you think? Names are important you know."

"I'm thinking I'm not too good at names. So, are you happy now?"

"Happy? All I know, Mosquito, is anyone who wants to be my friend will have to accept this complicated way I have been made. I finally understand I can't change who I am.

"But, Mosquito, I'm totally wiped out. I've never flown so far. So fast. I still shutter to think I was just inches away from getting eaten up by that dreadful Hen. Which is why I need to get some sleep. I'm totally exhausted. And perhaps you should catch a little nap too."

"No way, Butterfly, night is when I hunt and eat."

"Yikes! I totally forgot. My wings are so tired my mind got all muddled. I just wish you could find something to guzzle other than blood."

"I'm a Mosquito, remember? And I'm quite happy being me. Even if I'm stuck with these two ratty wings."

"Wings? Wings? I forgot to tell you, Mosquito, that bad feeling has left my wings. What do you suppose this could possibly mean?"

Striking his most somber scholarly pose, proboscis ahead and both wings spread, Mosquito wisely replied, "It's obvious to

"What am I? A Butterpillar? A Caterfly? I have the soul of
a Caterpillar tucked tight inside the beautiful body of a
Butterfly. This is the way I have been made. This is who I
am. But it's taken all my friends, even that dreadful Spider,
to help me see my complexity…is very much OK."

me, it can only mean one thing. That you are finally comfortable
being so much more than just a common ordinary Butterfly."

"For once in your life, Mosquito, you may be right. But
cross your ratty wings I don't have any nightmares about
that dreadful Hen tonight!"

"I will Butterfly. Sleep tight."

"Good night, Mosquito. And...Mosquito...even though you guzzle blood...I'm glad you are my forever friend."

"Me too, Butterfly. Me too."

"I'm very old. My roots go deep. I've heard it said I'm an ancient Tree. The endless winters I've seen are long and hard on me...standing stiff and cold without any leaves. Yet still I dread the coming of each Spring. When all kinds of creatures invade my bark and commandeer my leaves. All I can do is silently, patiently, wait for them to leave.

"The only one I've ever considered a welcome guest, and not a pest, is a dainty Butterfly. I can't keep myself from constantly watching her lavish orange wings. So I was puzzled to hear her say, one day, she is not exactly a Butterfly but a Caterpillar in disguise. Apparently, I've lived so long, I'm growing old in different times...when who we are, and what we are, is so much more than how we appear. It is our dreams and longings by which we are defined."

The End

About the Author

 I am not a therapist, an analyst, or a psychiatrist. I'm a writer, an artist, a mom, and a grandmother. And a self-educated expert on inner pain. I know from close up, from the inside looking out, that childhood hurts and insults cannot be brushed away.

My own case history predicted total disaster. As soon as I opened that Kindergarten door, the class bully was after me. My bullies changed over time. But the bullying never stopped, although it did become more subtle in that citadel of snobbery, Beverly Hills High. Without famous parents or popular students to vouch for me, I searched out lonely corners to cower in.

As an ardent philosophy major at UCLA, I loved all the fiery ideas burning through my classes. But the damage was done. My self esteem had been extinguished.

Was it my hair? My nose? My clothes? Why was I this social dud? The only aspect of myself I never questioned was my gender. Looking back, I'm certain the added weight of gender anguish would have easily crushed me.

There are many reasons, big and little, for kids not to like the way they were made. I wrote Butterfly's story to comfort and console, not just transgender children and young adults, but every adolescent who needs self acceptance and self esteem in the midst of despair.

As Butterfly said, "*There's so much more of me than meets the eye. At first I was sad. Then I got mad. But now I'm glad I'm not a common ordinary Butterfly.*"

Marilyn Bancel